ERIC STONE

THE ADVENTURES OF WANDERICH

AUTHOR

(YUVRAJ JAIN)

ABOUT THE AUTHOR

Yuvraj Jain is a 15-year-old storyteller with a brilliant academic mind and a boundless imagination. Passionate about weaving tales of adventure and courage, Yuvraj Jain embarked on the journey of writing this book to inspire readers to explore the depths of their potential. Outside of studies, [Your Name] enjoys diving into books, exploring new ideas, and creating worlds where anything is possible.

Table of contents

CHAPTER 1

THE INTRODUCTION:

Eric Stone, a 16-year-old boy with a brilliant and extraordinary mind, always curious for new and extraordinary things, asking questions which others didn't even dare to think about, and being first to any new discovery or adventure.

But, in his teenage everything started to feel stagnant, same routine following every day for several years, classmates who he felt the most exited with now started to feel boring too, no one understood that he yearned for new adventures far similar to his daily life. He wanted to break this daily routine. He always looked for ways to get engaged to something new that he has never experienced in his life, something that could ignite the fire of excitement in his heart once again.

One afternoon at his school, Eric found a book in his school library named "Crossing Antarctica" which was a story of will Steger who was also an explorer who also yearned for new and new adventures. He had actually crossed the

whole Antarctica without resupplies as he
started reading the book, he felt a deep
connection with will Steger. He admired people
like him very much after reading the book, he
thought "this is what I want to do in life, a story
that I can tell to somebody"

By the time he got home that day, he has
decided to accomplish what he wanted to do in
life. He couldn't wait any longer. He was being
called by adventure, and he had to answer.
Without hesitation, Eric grabbed a backpack and
packed it with some essentials like some clothes,
a sleeping bag, and enough food to last only a

day or two. He wrote a small note for his family that:

"I'm going on an adventure. Don't worry—I'll be back soon."

With that, Eric slipped out of the house, sat on his bicycle, and began just pedaling, not knowing where he was going.

He didn't even have a map, a plan, or even enough money to last the week, but none of that mattered to him. The thrill of the upcoming adventure was enough to keep him going.

Eric covered 50 kilometers by evening.

Exhausted, he realized he was in the middle of nowhere and there wasn't a single house or civilization in sight, just endless fields in the distance and a dark forest. With no better option, he decided to spend the night in the woods.

As he entered the forest, Eric got stunned and mesmerized by looking at the jungle, towering trees, their branches stretching high into the sky like giants guarding a secret. The air was cool and crisp, carrying the scent of like rain and wet leaves. While exploring, he stumbled upon an apple tree. The sight of the ripe fruit was a relief, he plucked few apples and savored every bite.

But something about the forest felt strange. The trees were very strange as they were gigantic as he had never saw trees like that, their roots twisting like hairs of the nature. Narrow, street like paths all around the jungle, almost as if they had been carefully crafted by human hands. Eric's curiosity clicked in his mind, and he decided to follow one of these paths, hoping it would lead him to something extraordinary, a place he has never witnessed before.

After wandering for what felt like hours, Eric realized he had no idea how to find his way back. He started to panic and decided to retrace his steps back, only to find himself going in circles. The forest, which had seemed so enchanting before, now felt like a prison.

As the night approached, Eric decided that he had no choice but to rest. He opened his sleeping bag beneath a tree and lay down, staring at the scenery above. The stars winked through gaps in the leaves, offering him a small sense of comfort.

But sleeping in the unknown wasn't very easy, In the dead of night, Eric woke up by a faint whisper. It sounded like someone was calling him by his name. With a chilled heart, he stood up and scanned his surroundings. With a frightened voice he asked "Who's there?". But the forest was silent. He tried convincing himself

that it was just the wind and nothing to fear
about, but unease was lying in his chest.

After only a few minutes, the whisper came
again, this time louder. Eric bolted upright, his
eyes were scanning through the darkness. That's
when he saw a glowing light flickering behind a
tree. Driven by curiosity, Eric got up and started
approaching the source.

As he was getting closer, he found himself
staring at a small, glowing pearl covered in moss.
Its light was mesmerizing, casting an

otherworldly glow that made the shadows dance. Eric hesitated for a moment before reaching out to touch it. But as his fingers brushed the surface, the pearl suddenly started flying into the air.

Mesmerized, Eric watched as the pearl began to fly away up in the air, as if leading him somewhere. Without a second thought, he started following it, weaving through the forest with the glowing orb as his guide. It started moving faster and faster, and just when he thought he'd lost it, Eric spotted it hovering near the entrance of a cave.

Breathing heavily, he stepped into the cave, he didn't feel any fear as his curiosity was on its peak. As soon as he entered, a loud rumble echoed behind him. He turned to see a massive rock sliding into place, sealing the entrance. Eric's heart was beating like a drum, but there was no turning back now.

The pearl's glow dimmed as it settled on a rock in the center of the cave. Eric approached cautiously and picked it up. For a moment, nothing happened. The pearl's light faded completely, leaving Eric standing in the dim cave with a slight feeling of disappointment.

he said "Is this it?".

But as he started to figure his way out, a sudden burst of energy stroked through him. The cave walls seemed to ripple and dissolve, and a bright light enveloped him. Eric screamed, overwhelmed by the sensation of being pulled apart and reassembled all at once.

When the light stopped, Eric found himself very
tired like he has travelled for several hours
without taking a break, he opened his eyes to
find himself standing in a completely different
world, The sky above was a deep shade of
yellow, with two suns casting golden light across
a landscape unlike anything he had ever seen in
his life. towering mountains floated in the air,
connected by shining bridges of light.

Strange glowing plants dotted the ground, their
colors shifting and pulsing like living rainbows.

Eric was not even able to say even a single word.
This was no ordinary place. It was a world

shinning with mystery and wonder, far beyond anything he could have ever imagined. For the first time in his life, Eric felt truly alive. The adventure he had always found for had finally begun.

As he gained some consciousness a voice from the sky said:

"Eric..., you are the chosen one to save our 'Wanderich'".

He wasn't able to fully understand the message but he knew it was the small start of something big which was going to happen later in his life, with this thought in his mind, he smiled gracefully.

CHAPTER-2

THE CALL OF WANDERICH:-

When the blinding light subsided, Eric's head was spinning, and his legs trembled beneath him. He squinted at his surroundings, his eyes adjusting to the soft golden hue that seemed to shine through the entire sky. Two massive suns hung in the sky; their radiant glow casting mesmerized him like he was in a dream. Towering, floating mountains floating in midair, as they were glowing with radiant beams of light, took his breath away. Everything around him seemed alive: glowing trees with translucent leaves hummed faintly, and streams of liquid light flowed like rivers through the terrain.

Eric rubbed his eyes in disbelief. "Where am I?" he muttered. His voice seemed to echo faintly, as if the air itself was alive and listening.

As he explored further, the ground beneath his feet felt soft yet firm, as though he was walking on a dense cloud. Strange creatures darted in and out of sight—small, glowing insect looking fireflies but larger and more fluid in motion. A massive bird with feathers that shimmered like polished metal flew over his head, letting out a call that echoed like a haunting melody.

Eric exploring in wonder, trying to make sense of this magical world. His initial fear was overtaken by curiosity, though a small part of him felt the creeping loneliness of being lost. He touched a glowing tree, its bark was smooth and warm, as if it was pulsing with energy. "This place... it's incredible," he whispered, a faint smile breaking through his disbelief.

But the smile didn't last long. His mind returned to the voice he had heard before arriving here: "Eric, you are the chosen one to save our 'Wanderich.'" The words echoed in his head, cryptic and heavy. Who had spoken? What was Wanderich? And why was he chosen?

Encounter with a Stranger

Eric's thoughts were interrupted by a soft whisper nearby. surprised, he turned to see a strange creature emerging from behind, a cluster of glowing rocks. It was about the size of a human, but its appearance was unlike anything he'd ever seen. Its skin shimmered with a faint bluish hue, and its eyes were large and luminescent, like pools of liquid silver. It had long, flowing hair that seemed to sway as though moved by an invisible breeze, and it wore a robe made of iridescent fabric that shifted colors with every movement.

"Greetings, traveler," the creature said, its voice melodic and calm.

Eric froze, unsure of what to do or say. "Uh...
hi," he stammered, taking a cautious step back.

The creature tilted its head, observing him with
curiosity. "You must be the one the Prophecy
speaks of—the one who has come from the
Otherworld."

Eric blinked, his heart racing. "Prophecy? What
prophecy? And who... what are you?"

"I am Lyra," the creature said, offering a slight
bow. "I am a guide of Wanderich, tasked with
aiding those who are destined to shape
wanderich's future."

Eric's confusion deepened. "I don't understand.
I didn't ask to come here. I just... touched

something, and now I'm... here. Whatever this place is."

Lyra's expression softened. "You stand in Wanderich, a realm of magic and wonder. Few from your world have ever crossed into ours, and those who do are not here by accident."

Eric asked. "So, I was brought here on purpose? If yes, Why me?"

Lyra gestured for Eric to follow. "Come, walk with me. There is much to explain, and suggested him not to wander here without knowing anything about wanderich. Wanderich can be as dangerous as it is beautiful."

Hesitant but Curious, Eric followed Lyra. As they walked, Lyra explained that Wanderich was a realm sustained by magic but is on the verge of collapse. A dark force, known as the Shroud, was spreading across the land, corrupting everything it touched. According to an ancient prophecy, a being from another world will arrive, having the potential to restore the prosperity and exclusivity of wanderich.

"But I'm just a kid," Eric protested. "I don't have any magical powers or anything. How am I supposed to help?"

Lyra paused and looked at him intently. "The magic of Wanderich is not wielded with tools or incantations. It is drawn from the strength within. Your presence here means that you have the potential, even if you do not see it yet."

A New Goal

As they continued their journey, Lyra led Eric to an unknown place where a strange, glowing monument stood. It was a circular stone platform, covered with runes that pulsed faintly with light.

"This is the Nexus," Lyra explained. "It is said to be one of the gateways connecting Wanderich to other realms and is the powerhouse of wnderich, it protects wanderich from unwanted threats like shroud. If you wish to return to your world, you must first restore the Nexus's power."

Eric approached the monument, running his fingers over the runes. "How do I do that?"

Lyra's expression grew serious. "The Nexus draws its power from the Heartstones—ancient artifacts which were scattered across Wanderich Into 5 pieces, unfortunately all of these pieces were captured by shroud which made him able to corrupt the world of wanderich. Each stone holds immense energy and is guarded by powerful creatures or forces controlled by shroud. To restore the Nexus, you must retrieve these Heartstones and bring them here and thus shroud will be over."

Eric took a deep breath, the weight of the task sinking in. "So... I have to find these stones, fight off whatever's guarding them, and bring them back here? And then I can go home?"

Lyra nodded. "It will not be easy, but I will guide you as best I can. Know this: the journey will test you in ways you cannot yet imagine. But within you lies a strength you have yet to discover."

The First Challenge

As night fell over Wanderich, the golden sky deepened to a rich tone of black, star-speckled indigo. Lyra led Eric to a sheltered grove where they could rest. A small stream of glowing water bubbled nearby, and the air was filled with the soothing hum of the forest's nocturnal creatures.

Eric sat by the stream, his thoughts racing. "What if I can't do this?" he admitted. "What if I fail?"

Lyra placed a reassuring hand on his shoulder. "Fear is natural, but do not let it consume you. Each step forward will reveal your true potential. Trust yourself, Eric."

The next morning, Lyra guided Eric toward the first Heartstone, said to be hidden in the depths of a place named the rama's Veil of Whispers. As they approached the its entrance, a soft wind swept through, carrying faint, ghostly voices.

"The Veil is treacherous," Lyra warned. "It tests not only your courage but your mind. The whispers you hear will try to deceive you. Stay focused, and do not stray from the path."

As they ventured deep, the walls seemed to close in around them, their surfaces shimmering with an otherworldly glow. The whispers grew louder, forming disjointed sentences that seemed to come from every direction.

"Turn back... You cannot succeed... This is not your destiny..."

Eric clenched his fists, determined to ignore the voices. But as they delved deeper, the path became more confusing, splitting into multiple paths that all looked identical.

"Which way do we go?" Eric asked, his voice tinged with panic.

Lyra closed her eyes, her expression calm. "Listen not to the whispers, but to the silence. The true path will reveal itself."

Eric took a deep breath, trying to focus. He noticed a faint glow coming from one of the paths—a soft, pulsing light that seemed to match the rhythm of his heartbeat. Trusting his instincts, he pointed to the glowing path. "That way."

Lyra nodded. "Well done. Let us proceed."

As they navigated the path, the challenges grew more intense. At one point, the ground beneath Eric's feet crumbled, and he barely managed to grab onto a rocky ledge. Lyra extended her hand, pulling him to safety.

Finally, after what felt like hours, they reached a cavern at the heart of the place. In the center of the cavern, surrounded by swirling currents of energy, was the first Heartstone—a crystalline orb glowing with an intense, fiery light.

But as Eric approached, a deafening roar echoed through the cavern. A massive, serpentine creature with scales that shimmered like molten gold emerged from the shadows, its eyes blazing with fury.

Lyra stepped back; her voice urgent. "This is your first test, Eric. You must face it alone."

Heart pounding, Eric gripped a nearby rock, his mind racing for a plan. The creature lunged toward him, its movements swift and deadly.

Eric dodged, narrowly avoiding its fangs. Remembering Lyra's words about inner strength, he focused on the creature's movements, searching for a weakness.

Noticing a vulnerable spot beneath its jaw, it was like there was no protection there and was only firm muscle fibers, Eric devised a plan. Using the glowing rocks scattered around the cavern, he created a makeshift slingshot and launched a shard directly at the weak spot. The creature roared in pain and collapsed, its body dissolving into a harmless mist.

Breathing heavily, Eric approached the Heartstone and picked it up. Its warmth spread through him, filling him with a newfound sense of confidence.

"You have done well," Lyra said, her voice filled with pride. "This is only the beginning, but you have taken your first step toward becoming who you are meant to be."

As they left the place, Eric held the Heartstone tightly, the weight of his journey ahead no longer feeling as daunting. For the first time, he felt a spark of hope—hope that he could rise to the challenge and uncover the true strength within himself.

CHAPTER-3

THE FORGOTTEN SANCTUARY

Eric stood outside the Veil of Whispers, the first Heartstone pulsing with light held warmly in his hands. The sensation filled him with newfound hope, but he also felt the weight of responsibility pressing down on him. Lyra reminded him that this was just the beginning, and the challenges ahead would only grow and become more demanding.

As they ventured deeper into Wanderich, Lyra revealed that the next Heartstone lay in an ancient temple known as the *Sanctuary of Shadows*, a place abandoned for centuries. Legends spoke of a guardian who had lost to the Shroud's corruption and now ruled the sanctuary, guarding the Heartstone with strong vengeful anger.

Eric was still recovering from his first trial, and was a little anxious. But Lyra's steady presence reassured him as they made their way through glowing forests and along shimmering rivers. The journey itself seemed alive, with the environment reacting to their presence. Flowers

bloomed at their footsteps, and fireflies formed
gentle patterns in the air as if guiding their way.

Discovery of the Sanctuary

By nightfall, the duo reached the entrance of the
Sanctuary of Shadows. The structure was
colossal, built from dark stone that seemed to
drink all the surrounding light. complex
carvings decorated the walls, depicting battles
between ancient heroes and the shadow beasts.
A heavy mist swirled around the entrance,
adding a ghostly atmosphere.

Suddenly surroundings turned dark and a small humanlike creature appeared in front of lyra accusing lyra of being obedient of lyra and many more things.

It warned eric that lyra would betray him.

Suddenly lyra held a sharp stone nearby and stabbed it in the creature's chest and the creature disappeared.

Eric was stunned by its words he suddenly asked lyra "what was it...was it telling the truth, are you an obedient of shroud?"

She replied with smile "she was kaelith, started appearing after shroud captured the stones.

Some say she is an eye of God and some say she is the soul of shroud. She was testing our courage and confidence."

Eric hesitated as they approached. "You are so courageous, do you ever get scared?" he asked Lyra, with a faint voice.

Lyra smiled faintly. "Courage is not the absence of fear but the strength to move forward despite it."

Encouraged by her words, Eric stepped into the sanctuary. Inside, the air was thick and cold, the silence broken only by the distant sound of dripping water. The walls seemed to shift and breath, as if alive and possessed with a dark energy. Shadows danced across the surfaces, forming moving images that made Eric's skin crawl.

The Maze of Shadows

The first challenge within the sanctuary was a maze designed to test his mental ability. Each corridor seemed identical, and strange whispers echoed through the halls, similar to those in the Veil of Whispers but more intense. Lyra warned Eric to focus on his instincts rather than his eyes or ears, as the maze was designed to exploit doubt.

At one point, Eric came across an illusion of his family calling out to him, pleading for him to return home. The vision pulled at his heart, but Eric remembered Lyra's earlier advice and pushed through, refusing to let his emotions cloud his judgment.

Eventually, he found a small, glowing sigil (a sign used in magic) etched onto a wall. When touched, it revealed the true path through the maze. Lyra applauded him for his determination, noting that the sanctuary was testing his emotional strength as much as his physical ability.

The Guardian's Wrath

At the heart of the sanctuary lay the second Heartstone, encased in a pedestal surrounded by black flames. Before Eric could approach, the flames converted into a massive, shadowy figure—a humanoid creature with glowing red eyes and claws that seemed to cut through the air itself. This was the corrupted guardian.

Lyra stepped back once again, leaving Eric to face the guardian alone. The creature attacked with relentless speed, its strikes forcing Eric to dodge and strategize at the same time. Using the environment to his advantage, Eric led the guardian into one of the glowing sigils, which momentarily weakened its defenses.

Seizing the opportunity, Eric used a shard of enchanted crystal Lyra had given him earlier to pierce the creature's chest. The guardian let out an agonized roar before dissolving into shadowy mist. The black flames vanished, revealing the second Heartstone.

As Eric held the stone, a wave of energy coursed through him, filling him with a sense of clarity and resilience. Lyra praised his creativity and adaptability, but she also warned that the challenges ahead would test him in ways he couldn't yet imagine.

A Glimpse of the Shroud

As they exited the sanctuary, Eric noticed the sky had darkened unnaturally. In the distance, he saw a massive, swirling storm—a indication of the Shroud. Lyra explained that the Shroud was growing stronger, feeding on Wanderich's magic and threatening to consume the entire realm.

Eric felt a renewed sense of urgency. He knew he couldn't afford to delay the fate of Wanderich by wasting time celebrating on his success

CHAPTER-4

PART-1

IS THE FRIENSHIP TRUE?

A Fractured Journey

After acquiring the second heartstone, its glow illuminated Eric's path through the thickening forest, casting long, flickering shadows across the ancient trees. The energy radiating from the stone was warm, comforting, yet strangely heavy, as if reminding him of the burden it symbolized. Every step forward felt both an accomplishment and a reminder of how far he still had to go.

Lyra led the way silently, her pale silver hair glinting in the light of the twin moons above. Her usual calm nature felt strained; she was looking frustrated from eric as she was avoiding Eric's questions. For a while, they walked in silence, their boots crunching over scattered leaves and roots that sprawled like veins across the forest floor.

Eric couldn't hold it in anymore. "Lyra," he said, his voice cutting through the silent. "The

Shroud... it feels closer, stronger, like it's breathing down my neck. Are we running out of time?"

Lyra didn't turn around. "The Shroud is always growing, Eric. But we can't afford to rush. Every Heartstone you claim weakens him and he getting angry...very angry. One misstep, and shroud can take over your soul."

The uncertainty of her answer unsettled Eric, and he in disbelief, gripping the strap of his satchel tighter. He hadn't forgotten how

Kaelith's words in the Sanctuary of Shadows still gnawed at the back of his mind. Lyra wasn't telling him everything, and he knew it

The landscape around them began to shift as they ventured deeper into the heart of Wanderich. The vibrant blues and greens of the magical forest dimmed, the bioluminescent flora fading to muted grays. The air grew heavy with tension, each breath feeling thicker, more labored.

"We're nearing the Grove of Eternity," Lyra said abruptly, her voice softer than usual.

Eric glanced around nervously. The forest had become almost suffocatingly dense, the trees pressing in closer, their gnarled branches forming a canopy so thick that even the moons' light struggled to break through. Glowing spores drifted lazily in the air, but they provided no comfort.

"What's so special about this grove?" Eric asked, his eyes darting to the strange symbols carved into the nearby tree trunks. They seemed to pulse faintly, as though alive.

"It's alive," Lyra replied, her tone laced with caution. "The grove is ancient, older than Wanderich itself. It has its own magic, its own will. It's a place of trials, designed to test the worth of those who enter. If we're to reach the third Heartstone, you'll have to pass its test."

Eric's stomach twisted. "Another test?"

"This one will be different," Lyra said. "It's not just about strength or wit. The grove will dig deep into your mind, into your memories and fears. It will show you things you don't want to see. And it will try to break you."

"Fantastic," Eric muttered, his sarcasm masking his growing apprehension.

Lyra stopped suddenly, holding up a hand. They had reached the grove's edge, marked by a massive archway formed from the intertwined roots of two ancient trees. The roots writhed slightly, as if breathing, and faint whispers drifted through the air.

"Once we step through, there's no turning back," Lyra said, her expression unusually serious. "Are you ready?"

Eric hesitated, his heart pounding. But he thought of the Shroud, of his family back home, of the responsibility he now carried. He nodded. "Let's do this."

Entering the Grove

As they passed beneath the archway, the atmosphere shifted dramatically. The air grew colder, and the light dimmed until it was little more than a faint glow. The trees inside the grove were taller and more twisted, their bark blackened and their branches forming unnatural shapes that seemed to reach for Eric and Lyra as they walked.

The whispers grew louder, forming fragmented sentences that seemed to come from everywhere.

Eric froze, his breath catching. The voices were painfully familiar, each one carrying the tone of someone he loved.

"Keep moving," Lyra said sharply, grabbing his arm. "It's just the grove. Don't listen to it."

But the voices only grew louder, more insistent. The trees around them began to shimmer, their bark shifting like liquid until they formed the outlines of people. Eric's heart dropped as he recognized the figures—his mother, his sister, his friends from back home.

"Eric," his mother's voice called, her figure stepping forward. "Why did you leave? Don't you miss us?"

"I..." Eric faltered, his feet rooted to the ground. "I didn't have a choice. I had to come here."

His sister's figure appeared beside his mother, her eyes wide with hurt. "You could have stayed. You didn't have to leave us behind."

"That's not real!" Lyra snapped, shaking him. "It's a trick, Eric. The grove is trying to distract you. Focus on me!"

But Eric couldn't tear his eyes away from the figures. They looked so real, their voices so achingly familiar. His hands trembled as guilt surged through him.

"You failed us," his mother's figure said, her voice cold now. "You're going to fail Wanderich, too."

"Eric!" Lyra shouted, her voice cutting through the haze.

Eric blinked, the figures flickering and dissolving into smoke. He stumbled back, his breathing ragged.

"Are you alright?" Lyra asked, her voice softer
now.

Eric nodded shakily, though he wasn't sure if he
believed it himself. "Let's keep moving."

Kaelith's Ambush

The path through the grove grew narrower, the
trees pressing closer together until Eric felt like
he could barely breathe. The whispers had

subsided, but the oppressive atmosphere remained, weighing heavily on his chest.

They reached a clearing where a massive, blackened tree stood at the center. Its twisted branches formed a canopy that blocked out the sky entirely, and the ground around it was bare, the soil scorched and cracked.

Standing before the tree was a figure cloaked in shadow, her armor glinting faintly in the dim light. Eric's breath caught as he recognized her—

Kaelith, the woman who had taunted them in the Sanctuary of Shadows.

"Lyra," Kaelith said, her voice smooth and mocking. "Back so soon? You must really enjoy these little reunions of ours."

Lyra's expression hardened, and she stepped forward, placing herself between Eric and Kaelith. "Kaelith. I should've known you'd show up here."

Kaelith smirked, her sharp green eyes flicking to Eric. "And you brought the boy with you. How sweet. Though I have to say, he doesn't look like much. Are you sure he's the one destined to save us all?"

Eric clenched his fists, stepping forward despite Lyra's warning glare. "Who are you? Why do you keep following us?"

Kaelith laughed, the sound rich and full of amusement. "Oh, the boy has spirit. I'll give him that. But you really should be asking Lyra that question, chosen one. After all, she's the one who hasn't been entirely honest with you."

"What are you talking about?" Eric demanded, his voice rising.

Kaelith's smirk widened. "Oh, didn't she tell you? Your oh-so-trustworthy guide here was once a loyal servant of the Shroud. She stood by its side, carrying out its will without question. But, of course, she conveniently left that part out, didn't she?"

"That's enough," Lyra snapped, her voice icy.

Kaelith chuckled, clearly enjoying herself. "Touchy, aren't we? Don't worry, chosen one. The truth always comes out in the end. And when it does, you'll see just how much she's been hiding from you."

Before Eric could respond, Kaelith stepped back into the shadows and vanished, her laughter lingering in the air like a ghostly echo

CHAPTER 4: PART 2

The Tree of Memories

The clearing fell silent after Kaelith's departure, leaving Eric and Lyra alone beneath the massive, blackened tree. The oppressive air of the grove seemed to thicken further, and Eric could feel the weight of Kaelith's words settling in his chest.

"She's lying, isn't she?" Eric asked, his voice quiet but laced with uncertainty.

Lyra didn't respond immediately. Her gaze was fixed on the tree ahead, her expression unreadable. Finally, she said, "The grove demands we move forward. Whatever questions you have will have to wait until we're out of here."

Eric frowned, but he knew better than to argue. With a nod, he stepped closer to the tree, its massive trunk looming over him like a dark sentinel. The bark seemed to shift and ripple, as if alive, and faint whispers emanated from its depths.

"What do we do?" he asked, glancing at Lyra.

Lyra gestured to the base of the tree, where a circular pattern was etched into the ground. It glowed faintly, its runes pulsing with a rhythm that mirrored Eric's own heartbeat.

"Step into the circle," Lyra instructed. "The grove's trial is for you alone. I can't follow."

Eric hesitated, his palms slick with sweat. "What if I fail?"

"You won't," Lyra said firmly. "You've made it this far, Eric. Trust yourself."

Taking a deep breath, Eric stepped into the circle. The moment his foot touched the glowing runes, the world around him shifted.

The Trial Begins

The grove vanished in an instant, replaced by a swirling void of light and shadow. Eric stood in the center of the void, his surroundings constantly shifting—images from his life flashing in and out of existence. He saw his mother's face, his childhood home, the school he had left behind.

A voice echoed through the void, deep and resonant. "Eric Stone, you seek the third Heartstone. But to claim it, you must confront the truths you hide from yourself. Are you ready?"

Eric swallowed hard. "I... I think so."

The voice rumbled with amusement. "Think carefully, young one. The truth is not always kind."

Before Eric could respond, the void around him solidified into a familiar setting—his family's living room. The warm glow of the evening sun filtered through the windows, and the smell of his mother's cooking filled the air.

But something was off. The room was too quiet, too still. As Eric stepped forward, he realized his family wasn't there. Instead, a figure stood in the corner, cloaked in shadow.

"Eric," the figure said, its voice a twisted echo of his own. "Why did you leave them?"

Eric froze. "I... I didn't have a choice. I had to come here. To save them."

The shadow figure stepped closer, its shape becoming more defined. It looked exactly like Eric, but its eyes glowed with a faint red light. "And what if you fail? What if all of this is for nothing?"

"I won't fail," Eric said, his voice shaking.

The shadow laughed, a harsh, grating sound. "You're lying to yourself. You don't even know what you're doing. You're just a scared little boy pretending to be a hero."

Eric clenched his fists, his heart pounding. "I'm not pretending. I've made it this far, haven't I?"

The shadow sneered. "Barely. And only because of Lyra. Do you really think you can do this on your own?"

Eric opened his mouth to respond, but the words caught in his throat. The shadow was right—he had relied on Lyra for so much. Could he really do this without her?

The void shifted again, and Eric found himself standing in the middle of a battlefield. Bodies lay scattered around him, their faces hauntingly familiar. His family, his friends, even Lyra—all of them lifeless, their eyes staring blankly at the sky.

"This is your future," the shadow said, appearing beside him. "This is what happens if you fail. Everyone you love, gone. Because of you."

"No!" Eric shouted, his voice cracking. "I won't let this happen!"

"Then prove it," the shadow said, its form dissolving into mist.

The Fight Within

The battlefield faded, replaced by a dark forest eerily similar to the grove. Eric stood alone, the whispers of the trees growing louder and more menacing. Shapes began to emerge from the shadows—twisted, monstrous versions of the people he loved.

His mother stepped forward, her face contorted with anger. "You left us, Eric. You abandoned us."

"I didn't mean to," Eric said, his voice trembling.

His sister appeared next, her eyes filled with tears. "Why didn't you stay? We needed you."

"I'm trying to save you," Eric said desperately.

The figures didn't listen. They lunged at him, their forms shifting into shadowy beasts with glowing red eyes. Eric barely had time to react, dodging their attacks as he scrambled for a weapon.

His hands found a fallen branch, and he swung it wildly, managing to fend off the beasts for a moment. But they kept coming, their snarls echoing through the forest.

"You can't fight us forever," one of the beasts growled. "You'll fail, just like you always do."

Eric gritted his teeth, his arms aching as he fought to keep the beasts at bay. He thought of Lyra's words—of courage being the strength to move forward despite fear.

"I won't fail," he said through gritted teeth. "I can do this."

A surge of energy coursed through him, and the branch in his hands transformed into a glowing sword. With renewed strength, Eric struck at the beasts, their forms dissolving into mist as his blade cut through them.

The last beast let out a piercing shriek before vanishing, leaving Eric alone once more.

The Third Heartstone

 The forest faded, and Eric found himself back in the grove, standing before the massive tree. The glowing circle beneath his feet pulsed with light, and the bark of the tree split open, revealing the third Heartstone embedded within.

Eric reached out and touched the stone, its warmth spreading through him like a comforting embrace. He felt a surge of strength and clarity, as though the doubts that had plagued him were being washed away.

Lyra stepped forward; her expression unreadable. "You did it."

 Eric nodded, his grip on the Heartstone tightening. "I'm ready for whatever comes next."

CHAPTER-5

THE LAST RECKONING

The Last Heartstone

Eric stood at the edge of the final battlefield—
the cemetery where Lyra's mother was buried. A
cold wind howled through the desolate
landscape, carrying whispers of the past. The
moon above was shrouded by thick clouds,
casting eerie shadows across the ancient
tombstones. The ground was cracked and

lifeless, as if the land itself had been drained of hope.

In the distance, atop a ruined altar, the last Heartstone pulsed faintly within a stone pedestal. But Eric could sense it—it wasn't unguarded. The Shroud's clone stood beside it, a figure cloaked in darkness, its form shifting unnaturally, its hollow eyes glowing like dying embers.

Lyra tightened her grip on her sword. "This is it. The last trial."

Eric swallowed hard, forcing himself to stay calm. "And the hardest one yet."

They stepped forward together.

The Guardian of the Grave

The Shroud's clone moved the moment they crossed the threshold. It spoke with a voice that echoed in Eric's mind, a voice that sounded eerily like his own.

"You've come far, but it ends here."

Without warning, the creature split into three, each form identical and equally menacing. Shadows coiled around them, taking shape into monstrous tendrils.

Eric barely had time to react as the first clone lunged at him, a blade of darkness forming in its hands. He dodged, rolling across the cold stone ground, and countered with a strike from his enchanted sword. The blade connected, but the shadow reformed instantly, as if it had never been struck.

Lyra engaged the second clone, her attacks swift and precise, but the creature mirrored her every move as if anticipating her strikes. The third clone simply stood near the Heartstone, watching with a sinister stillness.

"This isn't working!" Eric gritted his teeth, his mind racing. "They're not real, they're just shadows!"

Lyra blocked a strike, her expression tense. "Then we destroy the source."

Eric's eyes flicked toward the original clone—the one guarding the Heartstone. The other two were distractions, illusions meant to wear them down.

With a deep breath, he channeled the energy of the three Heartstones into his sword. The blade flared with golden light, radiating pure power.

"This ends now!" He charged at the real clone, ignoring the others.

The clone raised its shadowy blade to block, but Eric's sword burned through it, cutting straight into its core. The creature let out an unearthly screech as cracks of light spread across its form.

The other clones dissolved instantly.

With a final explosion of energy, the Shroud's clone shattered into nothingness. The dark mist dissipated, and the cemetery fell silent.

Eric collapsed to one knee, breathing hard. Lyra stood over him, her expression unreadable. "You did it."

Eric turned to the Heartstone, its light no longer dim but radiant. He reached out and lifted it, feeling the power course through him. The final piece was his.

Lyra's Truth

But something was wrong.

Lyra stood frozen, staring at the grave before
them. Her mother's name was barely legible on
the worn stone, yet it glowed with the same light
as the Heartstone.

Eric stepped closer. "Lyra?"

She turned to him, her silver eyes filled with sorrow. "I am the last Heartstone."

The words hit him like a hammer. "What?"

"The Heartstones aren't just sources of power. They are the essence of Wanderich's protectors. My mother was one of them. And so am I." She took a deep breath. "That's why the Shroud has been hunting me."

Eric's mind raced. "Then... if we use the Heartstones to defeat the Shroud—"

"I won't survive." Lyra's voice was steady, but her hands trembled. "The moment we activate them, my life force will be part of the magic that seals the Shroud forever."

"No," Eric shook his head. "There has to be another way."

"There isn't." Lyra smiled faintly. "This was always my destiny."

Eric clenched his fists, anger and sorrow battling within him. She had been lying, not out of betrayal, but to protect him from this truth.

The wind howled, and the sky above darkened.

The Shroud had arrived.

The Final Battle

The storm above churned violently, a vortex of pure darkness. From within, a figure emerged—Kaelith.

But she was no longer just Kaelith. Her body was fused with the essence of the Shroud, her form twisted and monstrous.

"You think you've won?" Her voice was layered, as if countless souls were speaking through her. "You are nothing without her."

Dark tendrils shot toward Eric, but Lyra stepped forward. She radiated light, her body beginning to glow with the combined power of the Heartstones.

"I was afraid once," she whispered. "Afraid of what I was. But not anymore."

She turned to Eric, placing a hand on his chest. "This is where our paths separate."

"No—"

She smiled. "Thank you for everything."

And then she stepped forward, merging with the Heartstones.

A burst of pure energy erupted from her form, expanding outward. The light consumed the darkness, tearing through the Shroud's corruption.

Kaelith let out a scream as the light engulfed her, her form shattering into dust.

The storm above collapsed inward, folding upon itself, vanishing into oblivion.

And then—silence.

The End and the Beginning

Eric stood alone in the graveyard, the final echoes of magic fading into the wind.

Lyra was gone.

The Heartstones had disappeared, their purpose fulfilled. The Shroud was no more.

Wanderich was saved.

But Eric felt no victory. Only loss.

As he looked up at the sky, something glowed in his hand. A small, luminous pearl—left behind by Lyra.

Her final gift.

A whisper drifted through the wind.

"Whenever you need to return... follow the light."

Eric closed his fist around the pearl, his heart heavy but resolute. He had a choice now—to return home or to stay in Wanderich.

But whatever he chose, he knew one thing.

This was not the end.This was only the beginning.

<u>NOTE</u>

THE RELEASE DATE OF PART 2
OF THIS BOOK WILLBE
ANNOUNCED AFTER 500
COPIES IN SALES ON MY
INSTAGRAM HANDLE-
YUVI.2510